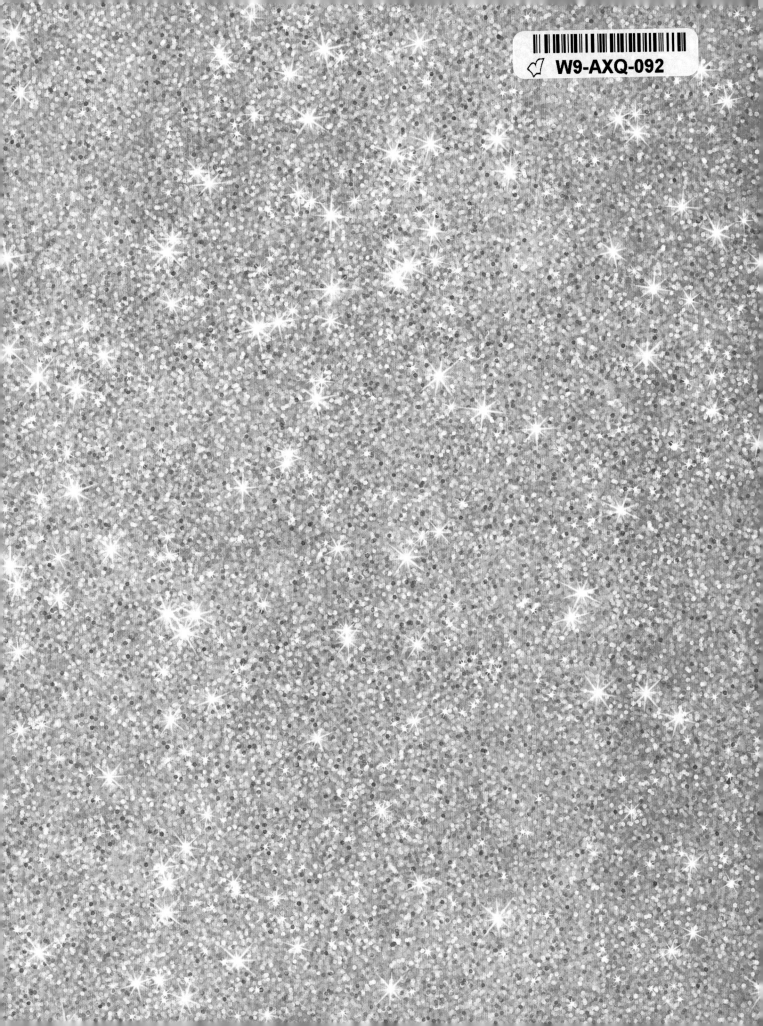

Adapted by David Lewman

Illustrated by Fabio Laguna

🐮 A GOLDEN BOOK • NEW YORK

DreamWorks Trolls © 2017 DreamWorks Animation LLC. All Rights Reserved. Published in the United States by Golden Books, an imprint of Random House Children's Books, a division of Penguin Random House LLC, 1745 Broadway, New York, NY 10019, and in Canada by Penguin Random House Canada Limited, Toronto. Golden Books, A Golden Book, A Big Golden Book, the G colophon, and the distinctive spine are registered trademarks of Penguin Random House LLC.

randomhousekids.com

ISBN 978-1-5247-7212-3 (trade) — ISBN 978-1-5247-7213-0 (ebook)

Printed in the United States of America
10 9 8 7 6 5 4 3 2 1

In the Bergen castle, King Gristle and Bridget opened a new holiday greeting card.

"It's from Poppy!" Bridget said, excited.

Gristle frowned. "Another one? If you ask me, those Trolls have way too many holidays," he grumbled. "Like, every single day!"

"I think it's nice," Bridget said, placing the card on the mantel next to the others.

"We do cool stuff, too!" Gristle said. "Remember all those awesome cards we sent back to Poppy?"

Meanwhile, over in Troll Village, Poppy opened a card from Gristle and Bridget. Inside was a picture of the two Bergens. Gristle was holding a sign that read MONDAY.

"Monday?" Poppy sighed. "That's not a holiday! It's like ever since the Bergens got rid of Trollstice—"

"Which was *good*," her friend Branch interrupted, "because Trollstice was all about eating *us*!"

"True," Poppy agreed. "But now they have nothing to celebrate. Nothing to look forward to." Her eyes widened. "Which gives me a GREAT IDEA!"

Early the next morning, Poppy showed Branch the scrapbook she'd spent the whole night making. It laid out her big plan: to give the Bergens one of the Trolls' holidays!

"HOL-I-DAY!" several other Trolls sang, popping up behind Branch and startling him.

"Looks like we're headed to Bergen Town!" Branch said, giving in to Poppy's plan.

After hastily preparing everything they needed, Poppy, Branch, and their friends climbed onto a Caterbus. They were excited to travel to Bergen Town and present their holiday ideas!

Branch was not excited when he saw who was driving the Caterbus: Cloud Guy!

"Oh, no," Branch groaned. "Not him!"

As they sped through the forest, the Trolls sang and danced to a rocking tune. They were having a great time!

Then Branch noticed that Cloud Guy was dancing in the aisle, too.

"Uh, who's driving the Caterbus?" he asked.

Everyone turned to stare at Cloud Guy just as the Caterbus . . .

. . . shot off a cliff and flew into the mouth of a giant worm!

"WORMHOLE!" Cloud Guy shouted.

The Caterbus twisted and turned through the eerie tunnels of the wormhole. Brightly colored lights flashed! The Trolls screamed!

"MWA-HA-HA-HA!" Cloud Guy laughed maniacally.

Through the windows of the Caterbus, Branch saw only black space outside.
The Trolls suddenly felt strange. As they looked at each other in amazement,
they transformed into plastic dolls! They all SCREAMED again.

Cloud Guy kept laughing his crazy laugh. "MWA-HA-HA-HA!"

Finally, the Caterbus escaped from the wormhole. It blasted out of the old Troll Tree and into the sky over Bergen Town, leaving a rainbow trail as it rocketed toward the castle.

The Trolls felt like their normal selves again and went back to happily singing and dancing. Then—*WHUMP!*—the Caterbus landed right in front of the Bergen castle.

Poppy led the Trolls into the throne room. Bridget was thrilled to see her little friend. "What are you doing here, Poppy?" she asked.

"We came to give you one of our holidays!" Poppy explained. "Hit it!"

Right on cue, DJ Suki started the music, and the Trolls joyfully presented Troll holiday after Troll holiday. . . .

GLITTERPALOOZA!

(Gristle got glitter in his eyes.)

TICKLE DAY!

(Bridget said Bergens weren't ticklish.)

LASERS AND FOAM DAY!

(Gristle got foam in his eyes.)

BALLOON SQUEAL DAY!

(The Bergens covered their ears.)

But the Bergens didn't like any of their ideas.

"Why don't we take a five-minute break?" Branch suggested.

Bridget whispered to Gristle, "I'm not so sure about these holidays. They're all for Trolls!"

Gristle took off his crown and shook glitter out of his hair. "Poppy's your friend," he said. "You've got to do something!"

"I'm trying to stop her, but she won't listen," Bridget sighed. "She's so *peppy*, that Poppy."

Just outside the throne room, Branch was huddled with Poppy.

"Poppy, you've done a great job," he said, "but it's a disaster!"

"What?" Poppy said, surprised.

"You know how you always say 'Go big or go home'?" he asked. "Maybe we should go home."

"Or," Poppy suggested, "we should go BIGGER!"

Poppy ran back into the throne room. She and her friends pumped up the volume and sang about many more Troll holidays: Epic Hug Ball Day! Shock a Friend Day! Express Yourself Day! Socks Day! Keep It to Yourself Day! Fireworks Day! Fuzzy Onesie Day!

"STOP!" Bridget finally cried.

The Trolls froze.

"None of this really means anything to us," Bridget said to her friend.

"Right," Poppy said, nodding. "How about Pick a Friend's Nose Day? Or—"

"Poppy, enough!" Bridget interrupted. "You're not listening to me! I . . . I think maybe you should go."

Stunned and hurt, Poppy turned and ran out of the room.

Branch ran after Poppy. He found her hiding in a nearby forest.

"I totally blew it with Bridget," she admitted. "I'm worried I just lost my Best Friend Forever . . . forever!"

"That's not possible," Branch said, shaking his head. "When you make a friend, it's a friend for life." To cheer her up, he started to sing. Poppy asked him to stop, but he kept going. . . .

At the castle, Bridget and Gristle were cleaning up.

"I can't believe they did all this!" Gristle complained. "I mean, why does Poppy even care so much about what we do?"

Bridget spotted a card on the mantel with a picture of Bridget and Poppy and HAPPY BEST FRIEND DAY! on it.

"You're right," she said. "Poppy does care. *A lot.*" That gave her an idea. "Hey! Maybe we do have a reason to celebrate a holiday after all! Come on, Grissy! We have work to do!"

HAPPY BEST FRIEND DAY!

Meanwhile, out in the forest, Branch was still singing to Poppy.

"I keep telling you to stop, but you won't!" she cried. "It's like you're not even listening— Oh. That was what I did with Bridget, right?"

Poppy finally realized that she had only thought about the things Trolls liked. She hadn't thought about what would make the Bergens happy.

Then she and Branch heard festive music in the distance. What was that?

Poppy, Branch, and the other Trolls ran through Bergen Town toward the music. When they reached the top of a hill, they saw something beautiful. . . .

The Bergens were celebrating a holiday! They had decorated the Troll Tree, and there was even a Bergen choir singing!

Bridget ran over to Poppy. "I'm so glad to see you!" she said.

"I'm sorry, Bridget," Poppy said. "I should have listened to you."

"That's all right," Bridget said. "Holidays are about celebrating the awesome things in life. So we're celebrating our friendship with the Trolls!"

The Bergens and the Trolls joined together to sing a happy song about celebrating their new holiday: Bergen-Troll Friendship Day!

"This is the best holiday EVER!" Poppy declared.